MOTHER FOX AND HER NAUGHTY CUBS, FOFO AND FIFI

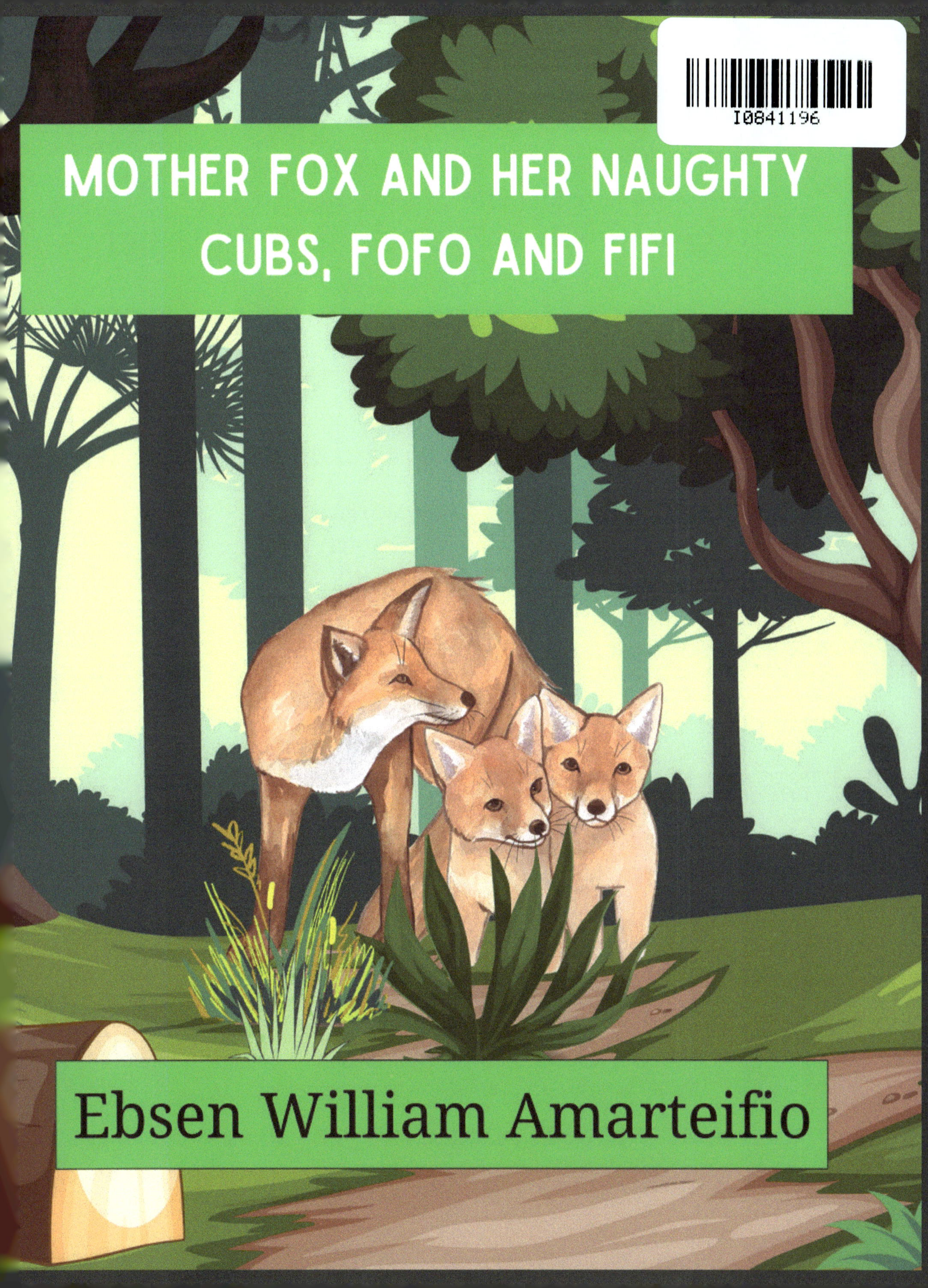

Ebsen William Amarteifio

LUNA GLOBAL MEDIA
Suncrest Dv. Melbourne, FL
+1 312 212 3899 U.S.
https://lunaglobalmedia.com/

MOTHER FOX AND HER NAUGHTY CUBS, FOFO AND FIFI

Copyright © 2023 by Ebsen William Amarteifio
All rights reserved.

No part of this book may be reproduced, stored in a retrieval system, or transmitted in any way by any means, electronic, mechanical, photocopy, recording or otherwise without the prior permission of the author except as provided by USA copyright law.

The opinions expressed by the author are not necessarily those of LUNA GLOBAL MEDIA the publishers of this book.

ISBN (Paperback): 979-8-9888550-2-6

Printed in the United States of America

Mother Fox had a very busy Friday night gathering food for her young ones. It was during the eighth week of the Corona lockdown. The spring, May weather was brilliant. It was like the middle of summer.

2

3

Mother Fox was tired, so she decided to have a short rest while her playful cubs, Fofo and Fifi remained safe by her side. Their lair, which is a resting or hiding place, was a spacious hole dug under the raised bushes by the side of a busy urban railway track. The front of the lair was so cleverly covered that none of the busy railway workers knew that foxes lived there.

Mother Fox might have had about
fifteen minutes' rest when she
suddenly woke up.

She could neither find Fofo nor
Fifi playing nearby.
She called out, "Fofo, Fifi where
are you?"
She continued, "You-hu-u-u-u, children,
where are you?"

Having called out a couple of times more, Mother Fox started to panic. When the cubs were only a few days old; their father went out for food but never returned. Mother Fox did not know what happened to him. She had no time to mourn the absence of Daddy Fox. Her two cubs were a handful. They always kept her on her paws.

8

Mother Fox was the only provider. She was a proud mother and very protective of her young ones although they were four months old. She cried out, "What can I do? Where are my little ones?"

Half-an-hour passed and still no sign of Fofo and Fifi. Mother Fox was beside herself with worry. She was in tears. She wondered and cried," What has happened to my dear little ones?"

Suddenly the leaves and branches covering the front of the lair were violently disturbed. Mother Fox quickly stepped back. She feared that her life was in danger. Her fear quickly turned to relief when her cubs romped past her into the back of the lair.

She made a huge sigh of relief; but suddenly asked, with a stern voice, "Where have you two been?"

Fofo appeared nervous repeating,
"We.....We....We .."
Mother Fox was angry and asked,
"You what?"
Fifi then answered without any fear,
"We went to look for food."
Mother Fox shouted," Where?"
Fifi answered, "The house at the
other side of the railway track."

14

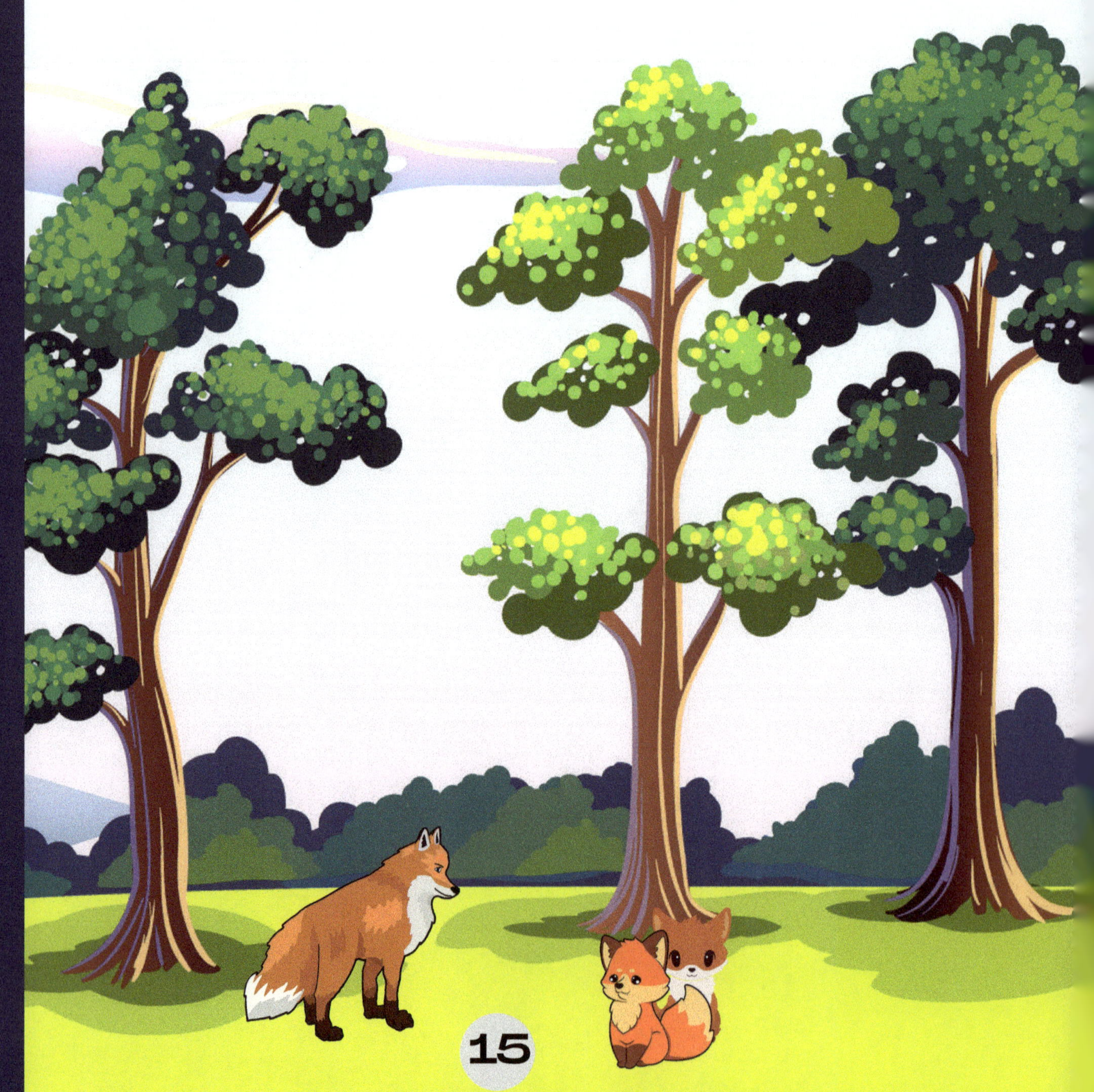

Mother Fox became even angrier and very fearful. She asked," You mean you crossed over the busy railway tracks?"
There was a moment of silence then Mother Fox continued, "What about if something happened to you both? I don't know what happened to your daddy about four months ago.
He also went out for food."
Fifi again had the courage and explained, "We listened for a long time, the ground was not shaking...."

Mother Fox was still angry and asked, "The ground was not shaking, so what?"

Fifi explained with more confidence, "But mum you told us that if the ground is not shaking, then it is safe to cross over because there are no trains coming. You even told us that it is easy to hear the railway workers whom you said talked too much and made a lot of noise with their tools."

18

Mother Fox agreed but added, "Children, yes I said all that but you are not old enough to go and find food on your own. I also know that for some weeks now the trains are not running as often as they did. Despite that it is still dangerous even for a grown up."

When mother Fox realized that she had their full attention, she continued, "I am your mother, it is my job to go out and get food for you."

Mother Fox continued with her lecture and asked," Come to think of it, didn't we have enough food last night and this morning?"
Fofo answered, "We did...........", But before Fofo could explain, Fifi stated, "Mum the problem is we are both fed up with the boring leftover cabbage and rotten fruit you give us morning, noon and night. You have stopped bringing us some meat and cheese."

23

Mother Fox was surprised and angry. She shouted, "You naughty little children, cheeky monkeys."
On hearing this, Fofo started crying. Mother Fox asked, "What are you crying about?"
Fofo answered, still crying, "I am not a cheeky monkey."
Mother Fox asked again," So what are you then?"

25

Fofo wiping her tears and with a bit of confidence replied, "But Mum it was only yesterday when you told me that I was 'a cute little fox,' now you are calling Fifi and me, 'cheeky monkeys. I'm not a monkey, I'm a fox. It is not fair."

Meanwhile Fifi was standing by with a broad smile on its face enjoying the drama.

Mother Fox then appeared to understand but turned to Fifi, "You are the naughty one. You have always led poor Fofo on to be naughty."
Having been told off, Fifi stopped smiling but Fofo appeared a bit better.
Fofo and Fifi remained quiet enough for Mother Fox to repeat some of the warnings and give more pieces of advice.

28

29

Mother Fox said," The ground shakes when the trains are approaching. It is still not safe when there are no trains because you are not old enough to go out for food on your own. In the big house at the other side of the tracks, where the shed is broken, there is a grumpy old man in the house always shouting."
Fifi then said, "We did not see any grumpy old man shouting."
Mother Fox quickly replied, "Keep quiet child and listen carefully."

Mother Fox then continued, " I don't think that grumpy old man is a nice man. I once jumped the fence from his neighbour's side. I fell on the grumpy old man's flowerpot.
His bin was not far off. He came out shouting and throwing his big arms about. He then threw a big stick at me. Luckily it missed and I escaped by the fence near the broken shed. So children, when you are old enough to look for food, don't go there."

Fofo and Fifi were very attentive and appeared a bit frightened especially Fofo.

Mother Fox continued," I have been getting you some food from either house of the grumpy old man's big house. For some nights now I have been getting nothing but cabbage and rotten fruit for you. I could go farther to the other houses for food and with some luck get some meat and even cheese. However, I do not want to leave you on your own for too long while I search for food."

Mother Fox then made a deal with her young ones, "Do we have a deal? I want you to behave yourselves and tomorrow night with a bit of luck, we shall have something different and nice for dinner."
Fofo and Fifi both replied, "Yes mum."

36

37

Mother Fox also promised, "In a few weeks you will be five months old. You will then be old enough to go out for food on your own. A few days before then we shall safely cross over the railway tracks a few times, and I will show you how to find food without disturbing people."
In the Foxes' lair, everybody was happy, nobody was crying; and nobody was angry.

Some moments later, however, Mother Fox asked her two young ones, "So what food did you get at the grumpy old man's house?"
Fofo and Fifi answered in unison, "Cabbage and rotten fruit."

There you have it!

Some Facts About The Fox

There are thirty-seven types of foxes, but only twelve belong to the group we call true foxes. The popular ones are the arctic fox, red fox, gray fox, fennec and the kit fox. Foxes are medium size mammals that belong to the same family as dogs. Foxes have a flattened skull, pointed nose and ears. Foxes have a long bushy tail which is sometimes referred to as brush.

Foxes are generally smaller than wolves, jackals and domestic dogs. The largest of the fox family is the red fox. The red fox weighs on average between 4.1 and 8.7kg which in pounds is 9 and 19.2lbs. The fennec is the smallest of the fox family. It weighs an average of 0.7 to 1.6kg which is 1.5 to 3.5lbs.

Foxes find their habitats in many places including woodland, high mountains, sea cliffs, sand dunes, salt marshes and even safe urban areas. They make their lairs (resting or hiding places) under tree trunks, hollow trees and under raised bushes along the sides of railway tracks.

The arctic fox eats lemmings, snow hares, seal pups and vegetables. It quietly follows polar bears and when it is safe eats the leftover from their kill. They store food for the winter in rock crevices and return during lean times to feed themselves. Foxes in general are very crafty hunters.

THE ARCTIC FOX - It is also known as the white fox, polar fox or snow fox. Their thick fur keeps them warm enabling them to withstand temperatures as low as minus 70°c. In the summer the arctic fox has a brown coat with a light belly. It turns into a thick white one in winter. The arctic fox does not hibernate like the polar bear. The females give birth in the spring. They live in burrows, with extensive tunnel systems.

During blizzards they are known to push their way through the snow to create shelter. The arctic fox has the warmest undressed skin of any animal in the arctic. Some of the places where it can be found are Canada, Greenland, Russia, Alaska, Norway and Iceland.

THE RED FOX- It is the largest of the fox family. It can be found mainly in North America, Europe, Asia and parts of South Africa. It has a bushy tail, pointed nose and ears. They live alongside humans in both urban and suburban arears. They live in burrows underground. They can also live above ground in hollows. They breed during the winter. The male fox supports the female (vixen) by bringing food for the family early spring.

During rearing, a non-breeding sister or a female from a previous litter lends a hand. This provides a valuable experience when it is time for that female to rear her own litter.

57

THE GRAY FOX - Also known as the Grey Fox, is known throughout North and Central America. It has silvery grey fur, a black tipped tail and reddish fur on its chest and legs. While other foxes have slit-like pupils associated with cats, the Grey Fox has oval-shaped pupil. It is about three feet long weighing usually between 8 to 15lbs. The Grey Fox regularly climbs trees. The only other animal in the canine family which climbs trees is the raccoon dog.

   THE FENNEC FOX - It is the smallest of all the foxes. It has very large ears which help transfer sounds of the smallest prey and also give off excess body heat. It can be found in the Sahara Desert, one of the hottest and driest places on earth. It is so used to the high temperature that, a drop below 68 degree Fahrenheit (20°c), makes it shiver.

61

IIt can also be found in the Californian desert, where it lives in holes. It sometimes lives in a cave. It runs faster than the cheetah. Besides fruits and seeds, the fennec fox's diet includes termites, eggs and lizards. They live in family units of a male, female and their young. Most foxes however, live alone.

THE KIT FOX - This can be found mainly in North America. It can also be found in South Western United States, Northern and Central Mexico. It has a slender body, a large head with large ears. The tail is long and bushy. The tip of the tail is black. It has the largest ears within the fox family. The large ears enable the Kit Fox to hear very well. The ears also help in releasing excessive heat from the body. A fully grown Kit Fox stands about one foot high. It weighs no more then 4lbs.

It feeds on rodents, rabbits, fish, bugs and small birds. The Kit Fox mates in October or early November. The cubs are born in either March or April the following year. There can be three to as many as fourteen cubs at a time to rear. Usually the lair or den is large enough for all of them to live together. The female remains in the lair feeding and keeping the young ones warm.

The male meanwhile is responsible for providing food for all the family. The young will come out of the lair with their parents when they are a month old. When they are five months old, they are considered to be fully grown, therefore ready to go out alone.

www.ingramcontent.com/pod-product-compliance
Lightning Source LLC
Chambersburg PA
CBHW041148300726
48978CB00017B/1431